This book belongs to:

____

____

Frogster Loudmouth's Tadpole Days

MAPLE PUBLISHERS

Written by: Mridula Mitra Vyas
Illustrated by: Arpita Chatterji

Title: Frogster Loudmouth's Tadpole Days

Copyright © Mridula Mitra Vyas

Written by: Mridula Mitra Vyas

Illustrated by: Arpita Chatterji

First Published by: Indic House Private Ltd.
2F Ballygunge Place East,
Kolkata 700019

First Edition: February 2018

Second Edition: February, 2021

ISBN: 978-1-914366-00-0

Published by: Maple Publishers
1 Brunel Way, Slough,
SL1 1FQ, UK

All rights reserved. No part of this book may be reproduced or translated by any form or by any means, electronic or mechanical, including photocopying, recording or by any information storage and retrieval system without written permission from the author.

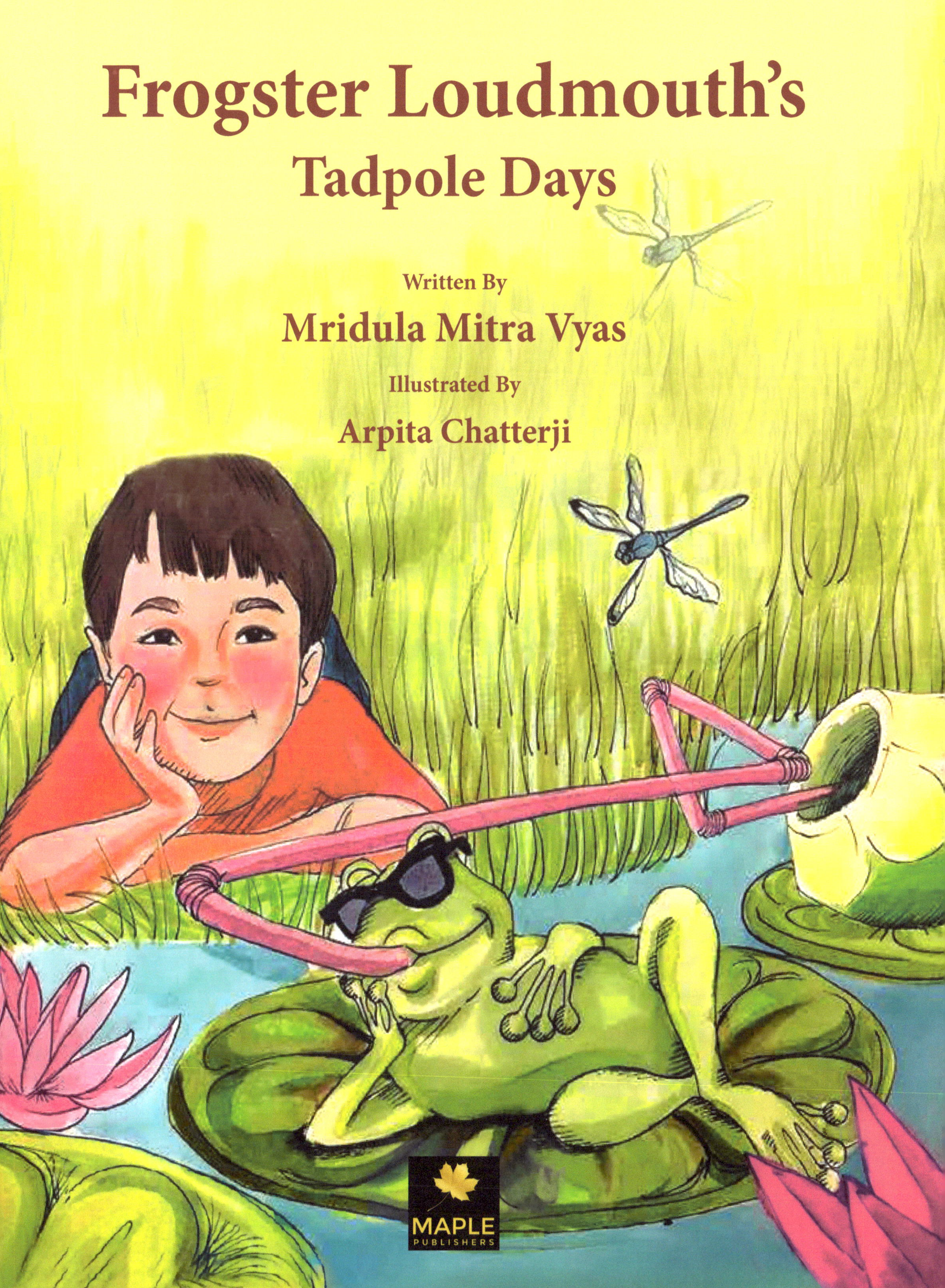

Frogster Loudmouth's
Tadpole Days
Written By
Mridula Mitra Vyas
Illustrated By
Arpita Chatterji
MAPLE
PUBLISHERS

It is summer time in a beautiful little town called Shamli in India. The air is thick with the smell of sweet, ripe mangoes. You can listen to the cuckoo calling from the mango grove all day long. At night the glow worms twinkle in the woods, while crickets chirp busily.

Next to the mango grove there is a pond, filled with pink water lilies. When the sky is blue, and the sun is bright, the water lilies are in full bloom. In that pond lives a frog. His name is *Loudmouth.*

In the summer Loudmouth loves to sit on a lily pad, bask under a mid-day sun and sip into the sweet water from a green coconut.

Across the pond is a large, red brick
house. In that house lives five-year
old *Cyrus* with his Dad, Mom, a
little Sister, a baby Brother
and their Grandma. Cyrus
has not seen his friend
Loudmouth in a while.

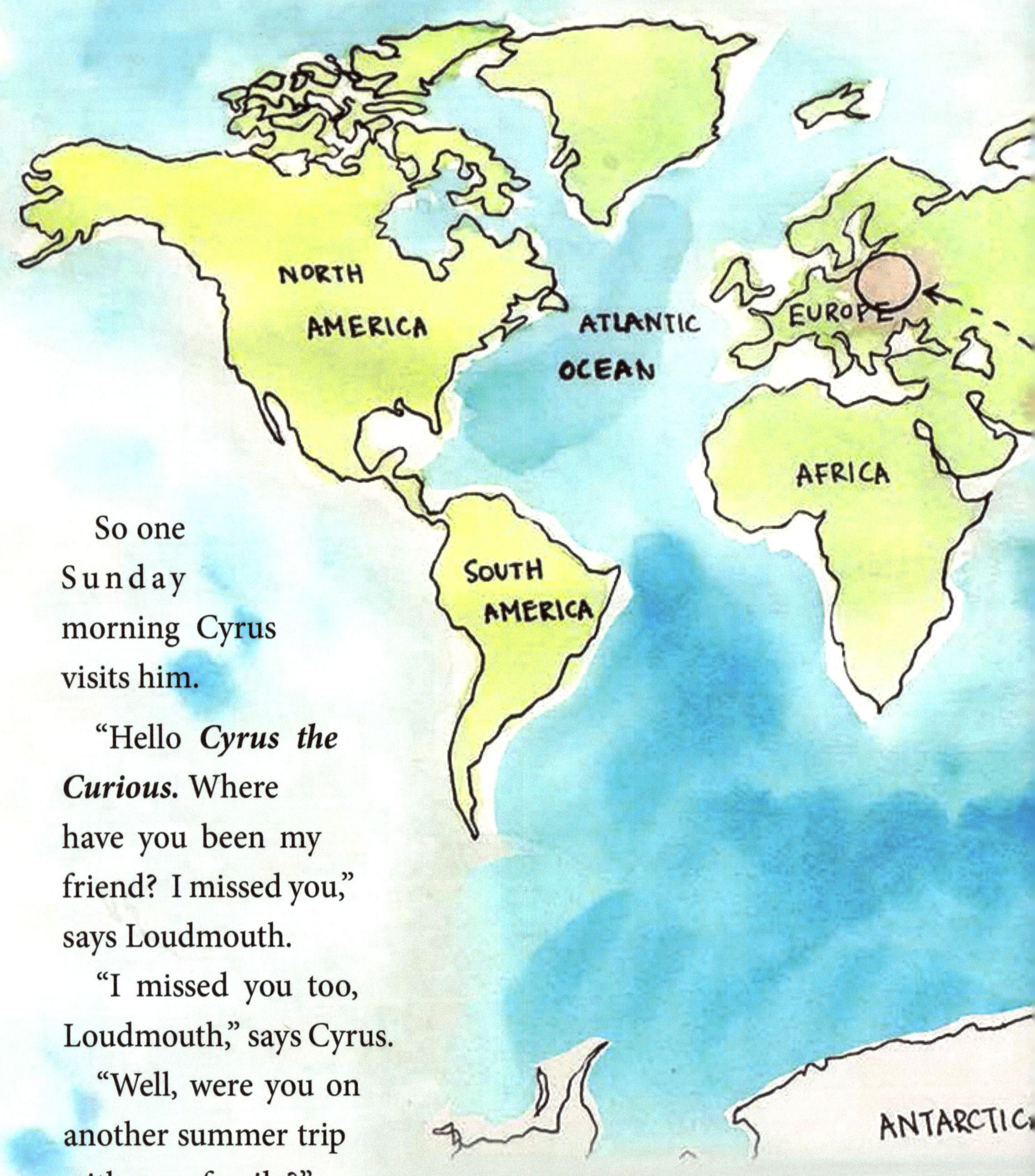

So one Sunday morning Cyrus visits him.

"Hello **Cyrus the Curious.** Where have you been my friend? I missed you," says Loudmouth.

"I missed you too, Loudmouth," says Cyrus.

"Well, were you on another summer trip with your family?"

"You guessed it! We went to Europe this year."

"You must have visited all the seven **continents** by now."

Loudmouth looks at Cyrus. "You know what a **continent** is, don't you?"

"Yes, I think I know. A **continent** is a large area of land where there are many countries with lakes, rivers, forests, deserts and mountains. No, I haven't visited all the continents yet, but I plan to when I grow up." Cyrus's eyes sparkle as he smiles.

"When I was at your age," Loudmouth pauses and looks a bit sad, "I used to know the names of all the continents, but not any more. Can you name them for me, please?"

"I sure can. They are Europe, Asia, Africa, North America, South America, Australia and Antarctica," Cyrus names them all in one breath.

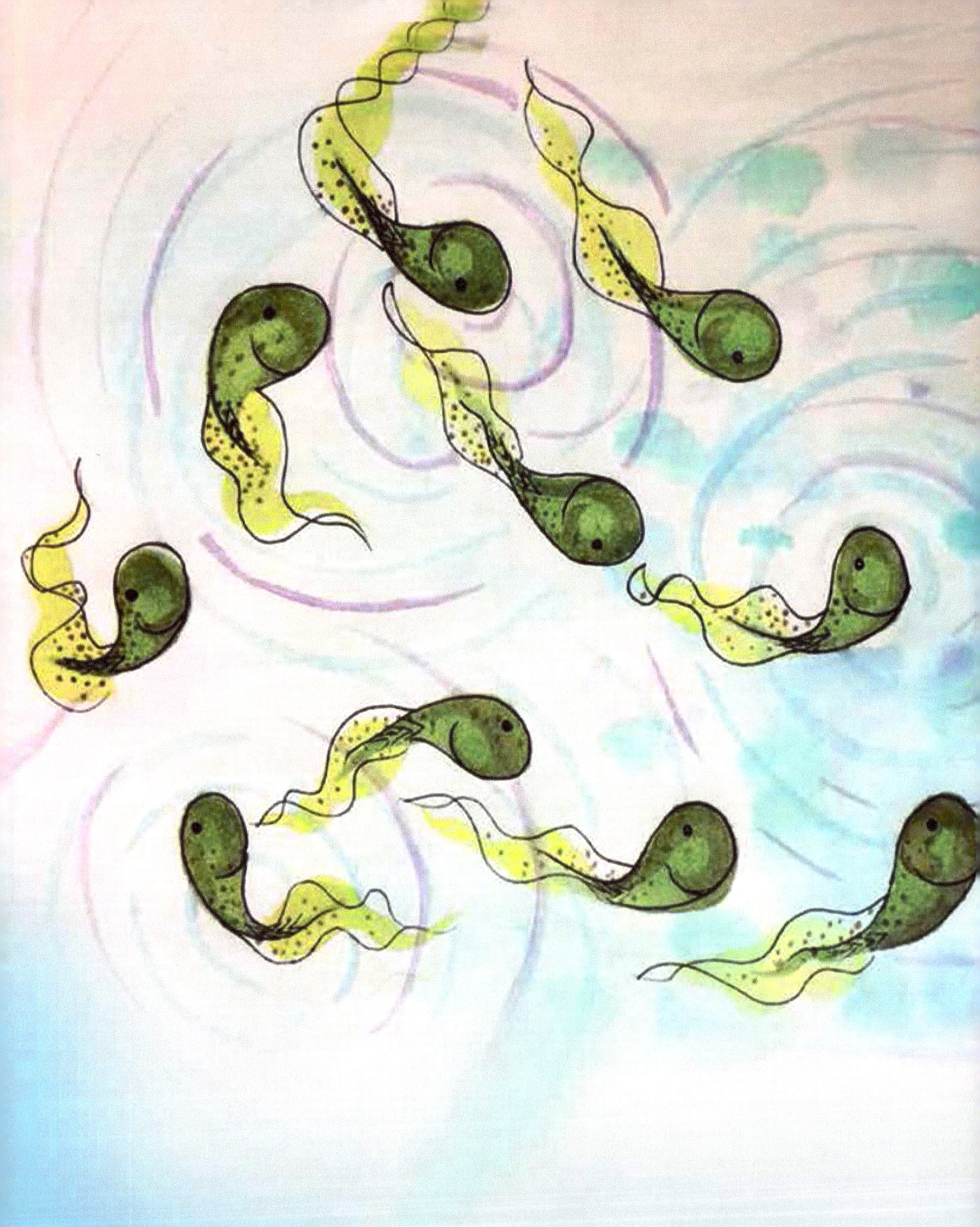

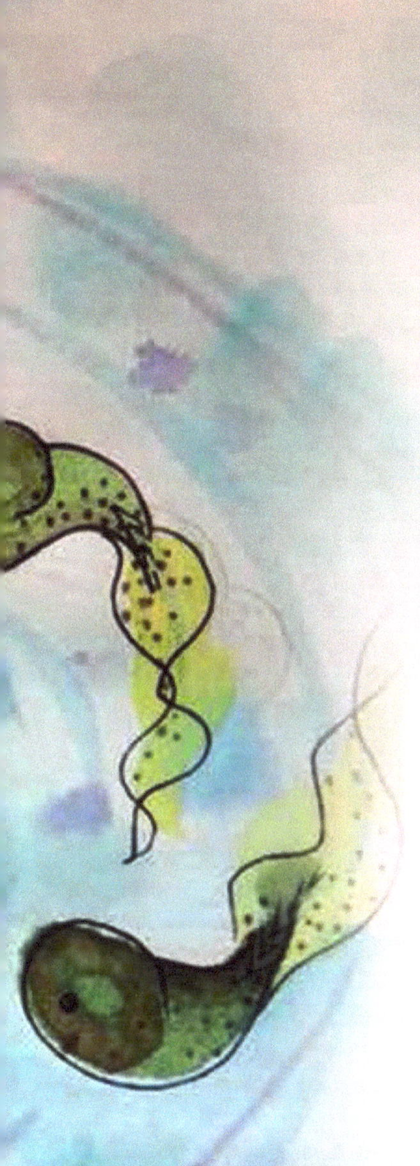

"I am so proud of you, my friend. You are a smart, young fellow."

"Thank you, Loudmouth. But today I like to know more about your childhood days. Where did you live? What was it like? Did you have many friends? Do you have a large family? Where are they now?" Cyrus wanted to know everything about him.

"In that case, my friend, Cyrus the Curious, let me tell you the story of my *tadpole* days. As you know a baby frog is called a *tadpole*. By the way, I like to call the story of my childhood days *A Blessing in Disguise.*"

"What does *A Blessing in Disguise* mean?" Cyrus asks.

"Wait till you listen to my story. You will know by then what it means."

Loudmouth takes another sip into his green coconut, clears his throat loudly and begins.

"Before I go into the story, I have to tell you a little bit about my family. Besides Papa-frog and Mama-frog, we were a dozen tadpoles, I mean baby frogs.

9

"I was not even an inch long and breathed through my **gills** then."

"So how do you breathe now?" Cyrus sounds curious.

"Just like you do, through my lungs, so as I was saying," continues Loudmouth, "it was when I had a long tail and no legs." Then after clearing his throat, Loudmouth continues.

"There were also other frog families in our neighborhood, you see. They were the snooty Sea-frogs and the Tree-frogs. But, we hardly ever saw them."

"Why do you think they were snooty?" Cyrus asks.

"Because the Sea-frogs, who lived by the sea, not too far from where we lived, thought they were a part of a bigger world than we were. The Tree-frogs lived high up on the trees, so they felt they had a better view of the world below where we lived."

"But that should not make them snooty." Cyrus says.

Sea Frog
11

Pond Frog
12

"Exactly, **all frogs are born equal** wherever we may live."

"Yes, just as **all children are born equal,** as my dad says."

"Your dad is a wise man, my friend."

"Yes he is."

"So our family of Pond-frogs was a happy bunch. We spent the summer together swimming in the pond. As it happened, the mosquitoes and the flies also shared our pond. Especially during the monsoon, when heavy rain filled our pond to the brim, the flies and the mosquitoes laid their eggs in thousands. They always floated on the surface of the pond. It was the greatest time of the year for us," says Loudmouth with an ear-to-ear grin. "So the Mama-frogs and the Papa-frogs ate mosquito eggs for breakfast every morning."

"And what about you and all your brothers and sisters, what did you all eat?" Cyrus asks. "Didn't your Mama also give you all some eggs for breakfast?"

"Oh! No," Loudmouth's eyes roll like a pair of white marbles behind the dark glasses. "We were on tadpole-food then."

"So tell me, how was your tadpole-food like?" Cyrus asks.

"Something like your….. you know….. hmmm…." Loudmouth snaps his fingers trying to remember the word. Then, all of a sudden, he excitedly hops on to another lily pad as the word suddenly springs into his head, "Aha, I know something like your baby-food, but ours are made of plants."

14

"So what do you eat now?" Cyrus asks.

"Now I eat all kinds of food— from spooky spiders, crunchy crickets, slimy slugs to soft tender worms and insects…. yummy… yum." Little Cyrus can see Loudmouth almost drooling at the thought of food.

"Loudmouth, tell me something," says Cyrus, "did you always enjoy eating all those worms and slugs and crickets?"

"Yes dear, from the day I learned to catch them with my tongue sticking out, I would quickly snap at those light-footed creatures. They are especially delicious when they are young and crisp. But you have to be a good snapper. They are very swift."

"What about slugs?" Cyrus asks.

"Oh! Those slow-footed, slimy creatures make easy prey for anyone."

Loudmouth chuckles as he leans back on the lily pad. He flaunts his hunting skill and all his clever tricks. "Let me tell you they are really good and juicy and surely a mouthful when they are plump."

"And worms?" Cyrus asks.

"Worms are always yummy, yummy." Loudmouth drools. "You can always grab a few of those with every slurp. Especially in the monsoon when nature is sweet and *bountiful,* it is like one big feast for us. Oh! Dear, only if you knew what you are missing."

"What does *bountiful* mean?" Cyrus asks.

"It means plenty, my dear friend." Loudmouth answers.

"Yes, I suppose I would miss," says Cyrus, "hmmm….only if I was a frog, but I am not. I love French Fries, Pizzas, Cakes, French Toasts, Ice Creams and Lollypops."

"You are probably right, my friend, I have to agree with you. But I couldn't enjoy Ice Cream like you do. I know it would make me hoarse," Loudmouth chuckles.

If there is one thing he loves to croak about, is his "golden voice" as he calls it.

"So soon after breakfast," continues Loudmouth with a great big smile, "we would all swim to the edge of the pond and scatter ourselves around, sunbathing." Then with a heavy sigh he continues. "Sadly enough, not all of us would return home."

"Why not?" Cyrus asks.

"It's because of the snakes. They are our greatest enemies. They slither along the edge of the water. Or hide behind the tall water weeds, waiting to make a hearty meal out of us." Another heavy sigh escapes Loudmouth's chest.

His face turns pale green as he remembers all his friends and relatives he lost.

"I remember Bigmouth, Tinytale, Greenspot, Longleap and so many more lives taken away by those cunning, cold-blooded creatures." Just then Loudmouth removes his dark glasses to wipe his teary eyes with his handkerchief.

18

19

"Also what upsets me is…" Loudmouth's eyes almost bulge out of his sockets, "when some humans eat fried frog legs! Now quite honestly I think that is disgusting! As a loyal and active member of our pond, I might take it up to your President some day." Cyrus can tell Loudmouth is angry. The color of his skin turns darker than usual.

"Yes, you are quite right. I don't think I could ever take a bite out of your…. excuse me…. I mean…. you know what I mean." Cyrus looks at Loudmouth.

"Thank you, my friend, you are so very kind. Anyways, as I was saying…."

By now the color of Loudmouth's skin softens.

"Of course, as you know, we didn't believe in a quiet life," says Loudmouth with a sniff. "Late in the evenings, usually after a heavy rain, the bullfrogs would begin to croak and continue all through the night. Having to put up with our

loud and
powerful
croaking,
night after
night, our
neighbors
got fed up. So
guess what they did to
us?" Loudmouth looks at Cyrus with a serious face. "They decided
to get rid of us!"

Cyrus feels sorry for Loudmouth and for all his family and friends.
"It was not fair to us," continues Loudmouth. "after all, we *inhabited*
the earth long before the humans came along."

"Excuse me, what does *inhabited* mean?" Cyrus asks.

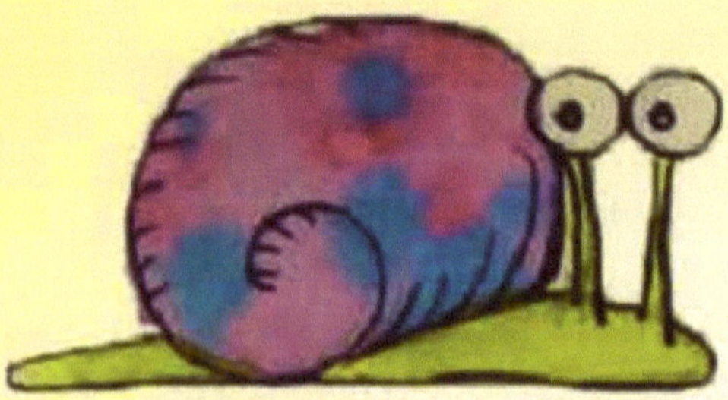

"I am glad you asked. Good for you! No wonder I call you **Cyrus the Curious.** We never learn if we do not ask questions, you see." Then after clearing his voice again Loudmouth explains. "Quite simply, it means to belong to a certain place from a long, long time where not only you but your father, and your grandfather and your great-grandfather lived and raised their families. So if you can believe it, we frogs have been living on this earth long before the humans came along."

"But how do you know that?" Cyrus asks.

"Good question! One of your very famous men by the name of Charles Darwin," Loudmouth removes his pair of dark glasses from his face, wipes it clean with his handkerchief and puts it back over his flat nose as he speaks, "Charles Darwin visited islands in the far corners of the world, studied all about animals and birds and humans

and wrote about how life *evolved* on earth.”

“What does *evolved* mean?” Cyrus asks.

“Well….. hmmm….Let me see if I can put it to you without confusing you.” Loudmouth snaps his fingers and hops from one lily pad to another until he finds the answer. “Aha, it means we came into this world slowly and gradually changing from one form of life to another over millions and millions of years.”

“I get it,” says Cyrus excitedly. “You evolved as a frog, a long time ago from some other form of life. Then after millions and millions of years we humans evolved also from some other form of life. WOW! When I grow up, surely I‘m going to read all about Charles Darwin and everything he wrote. I can’t wait to grow up so I can visit those islands and learn how life evolved on earth. Thank you for sharing it with me, Loudmouth.”

"You are most welcome, Cyrus the Curious. Now, to go back to my story, the children in our old neighborhood loved us. Especially with our lovely little tails I suppose we looked very cute." Loudmouth shakes with laughter.
"So during the summer

vacation, every afternoon they gathered around the pond and watched
our elders take the famous leap. But their parents decided to get rid
of us. So one sunny morning when the Pond frogs were having their

breakfast, a huge truck loaded with mud rattled over the edge of our
pond. The loud engine shrieked and frightened us all out of our wits.
Then there came one more truck... after another... and then another...
and another. All morning they unloaded heaps and piles of mud. Soon
our beautiful home next to the mangrove swamp in the East Coast of
India was filled with nothing but mud."

"So our Papa-frogs and Mama-frogs quickly gathered around and talked on the very important question of where we can find another clear water pond so we can live happily together again. Then after a long talk they decided to take a chance. So we left for the famous lake on the West Coast of India at the foot of the famous Toad Rock. That was to be our home if we would ever find it. Personally, I feel our parents were getting a bit too *ambitious* and *adventurous* as well."

"E-x-c-u-s-e me, what do those words mean?" Cyrus asks.

"You mean **ambitious** and **adventurous**? Hmmm…. let me see. I'd say **ambitious** means when one wants to do something great or somehing grand. Something that makes everyone wonder! Now, **adventurous** means something bold, brave and daring, something out of the ordinary. Like our elders who wanted to travel far in search of that famous lake, a place where no one from our pond has ever been. To me that sure was **adventurous**."

"I think so too." Cyrus agrees with Loudmouth.

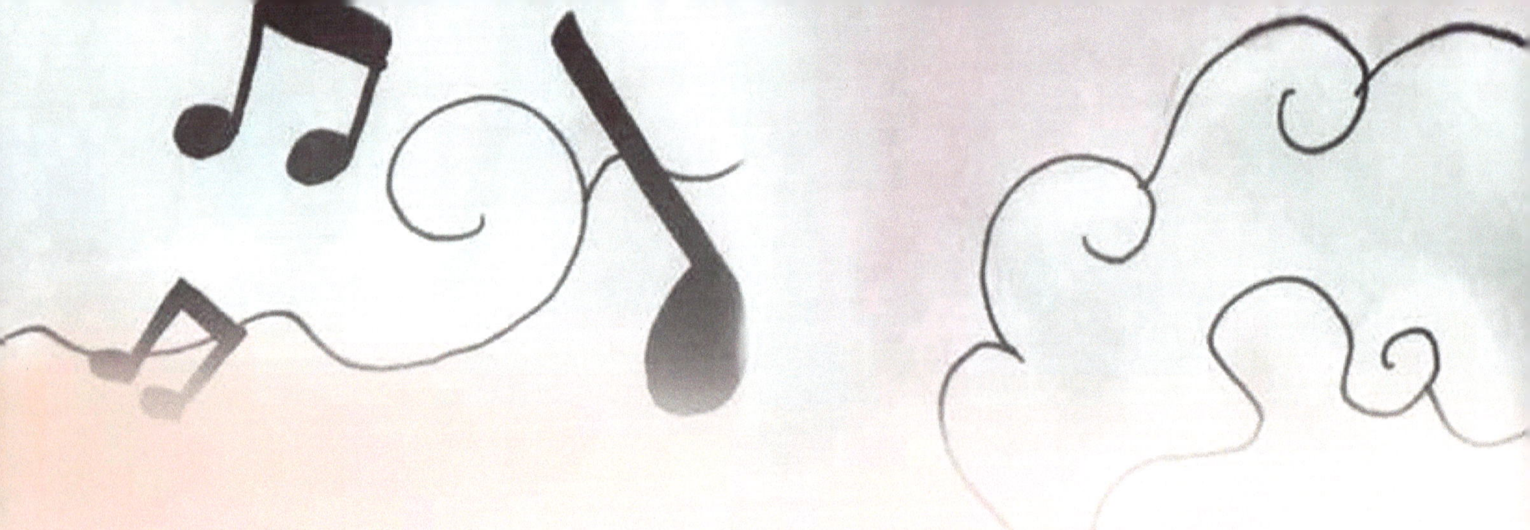

"So, as I was saying, before the humans buried us alive under a pile of mud, we sprang up on our feet. Then we hopped on a train and off we went in search of our new home. The train puffed out clouds of smoke. It whistled away merrily and rushed its way through deep valleys and dark forests. Every now and again we looked out the window. We wanted to see how far we were from our new home. I suppose we were getting a bit restless too. So our Papa frogs and Mama frogs began to sing. Soon we too were singing along with them."

"Loudmouth, would you mind singing that song for me?" Cyrus asks with a big smile.

"Oh! No not at all. I will be delighted to sing that song for you." Loudmouth clears his throat again. "But as you know I have a slight cold. So you must excuse me, if I should sound like a *frog in my throat* as the humans like to say! Haaa…Haaaa…. Haaaa…." Loudmouth and Cyrus burst out laughing. "Ok, here's how it goes."

"We are a bunch of beautiful green *amphibians*.

In case you are wondering what it means.

We are creatures that can live both on land

And in water."

Loudmouth suddenly stops singing. He takes off his dark glasses and looks at Cyrus. With his eyes bulging out, he says,

"And would you believe it! Before we could sing any further, we heard a loud CRRREEEK and a CRRRAK and a CRRRRASH!!!"

"And what do you know! Out of the window and into the pond jumped all of us, the young ones and the old ones."

"HURRAY! WE FOUND OUR HOME!! The elders yelled." Loudmouth continues his story, "Then hurriedly all the Papa frogs and

31

32

the Mama frogs got together once again and talked. The next thing we did was to see if any humans lived nearby. With a few exceptions like yourself, humans neither have the tolerance nor the taste for good *frog music*. But luckily you are our only neighbor and a true friend. Since our pond is so close to a mango grove, only birds, bees and butterflies flutter around happily. The water tastes sweet and looks as clear as a piece of glass. We fell in love with our new home. Now, you see, if the bridge had not broken and our train had not fallen into the pond who knows where we would be today. I think we would be still looking for that famous lake and not have a home of our own yet. So this was a *Blessing in Disguise*."

"Now I know what it means!" Cyrus screams with joy. "When something bad turns out to be something really good at the end, it is called a *Blessing in Disguise*."

"You are right my friend." Loudmouth takes a few leaps. He always does that when he is too happy to contain himself. "After we settled down in our new home we gathered around and sang the rest of our favorite song. This is how it goes—

'In the summer we love to
swim in a pond

Or in a puddle of
rainwater

And *hibernate* all
through winter.

H-I-B-E-R-N-A-T-E

Do you know what it
means?

It means we live
under the ground.

And we breathe
through our skin.

TRA LA LA LA LA'...

get it my friend!"
Loudmouth keeps on
singing.

"Loudmouth, thank
you for the beautiful story.
Thank you for the lovely

song you sang for me. Now I must run home and tell the story to my sister and my brother. But I must not forget to thank you for those new words and all that I learned about evolution today. So, see you later, Loudmouth."

"You are welcome and see you soon, my dear friend," says Loudmouth. "By the way, you can call me Frogster Loudmouth. Fr. for Frogster, just as Mr. for Mister."

"Oh, I sure will. You have a great day Fr. Loudmouth."

"You too my friend Cyrus the Curious."

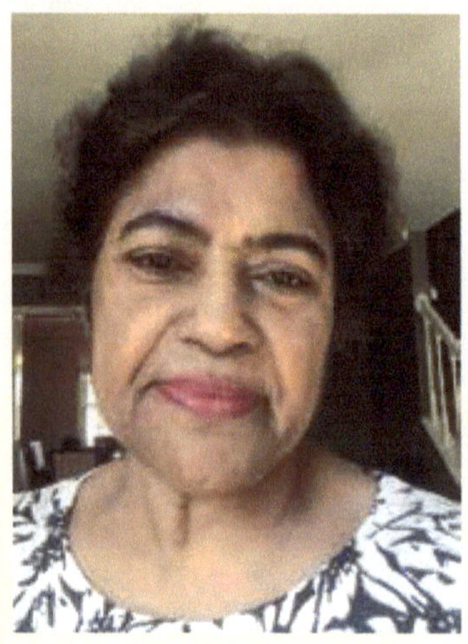

Author, Mridula Mitra Vyas, is also the author of *A Wounded Tigress.* She began her career as a journalist in India and later worked as a Technical Writer for a Federal Agency in Washington, DC.

Ms.Vyas, a Poet, Playwright and a Novelist, pledges to donate **50%** of the sale from her books to children in distress through UNICEF, UNHCR, Artists United against Childhood Hunger and a few more.

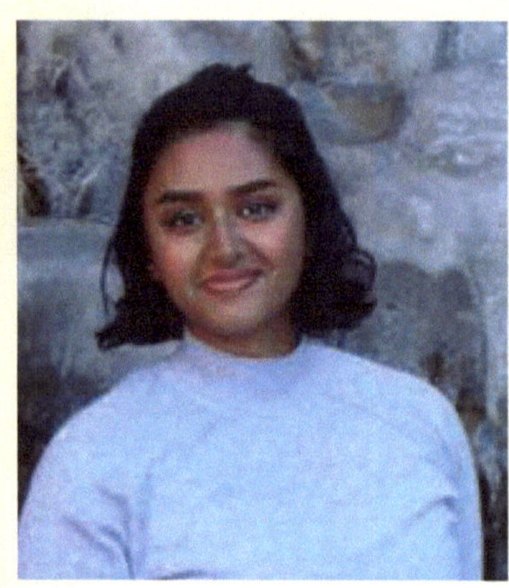

Illustrator, Arpita Chatterji, works with video art as a second year student of Kinetic Imaging at Virginia Commonwealth University. Nineteen-year old Arpita aspires to animate and direct films in the future.

Children's Books to be published soon:

◆ The Snowman and the Sunshine in Switzerland
◆ Actions Speak Louder
◆ Eva's Unselfish Love
◆ Crystal's Dream

www.ingramcontent.com/pod-product-compliance
Lightning Source LLC
Chambersburg PA
CBHW042126030726
47599CB00002B/358

9 781914 366000